THE GOLEM

THE GOLEM

A VERSION BY
BARBARA ROGASKY

ILLUSTRATED BY
TRINA SCHART HYMAN

HOLIDAY HOUSE · NEW YORK

Text copyright © 1996 by Barbara Rogasky
Illustrations copyright © 1996 by Trina Schart Hyman
All rights reserved
Printed in the United States of America
First Edition
Library of Congress Cataloging-in-Publication Data
Rogasky, Barbara.
The golem: a version / by Barbara Rogasky: illustrated by Trina
Schart Hyman. — 1st ed.
p.   cm.
Summary: A saintly rabbi miraculously brings to life a clay giant who
helps him watch over the Jews of sixteenth-century Prague.
ISBN 0-8234-0964-3
1. Golem—Juvenile fiction.   [1. Golem—Fiction.   2. Jews—
Czechoslovakia—Fiction.]   I. Hyman, Trina Schart, ill.
II.   Title.
PZ7.S62553Go   1996   94-13040   CIP   ACr96
[Fic]—dc20

To Deborah Jones, for all the reasons she knows
and others besides.

B R

For Truth is alive, dwelling somewhere, never weary.
And all of mankind is needed to liberate it.

—GERSHON SCHOLEM

Contents

CONTENTS

THE GOLEM

The Lion

A long time ago, there lived a great and learned man who was the chief rabbi of all the Jews in the city of Prague. His name was Judah Loew, which means the lion. So deep was his faith, it was believed he could perform miracles. He was very wise and kind, and the Jews came to him for advice and help whenever they needed it.

The life of the Jews was very hard. The emperor permitted them to live in only one part of the city, the ghetto, which they were forbidden to leave after sundown. The ghetto's streets were narrow and dark, and twisted and turned crazily. The houses were so old that some of them actually leaned out over the street. The rooms were small and crowded. Most of the Jews were poor, very poor.

Jews sometimes worked with the Christians of Prague and the other way around. They did business with each other and traded together in the marketplace. But mostly they kept separate. The life of the Jews was mysterious and strange to the others. Maybe because of this, many of the townspeople distrusted the Jews, and some hated them.

The hatred went so deep that lies were made up about them. Terrible lies, some of them, spread to give an excuse to arrest Jews or even to start a bloody pogrom, a massacre of innocent Jews.

Why? Who knows why?

Maybe just because they were Jewish. That was enough.

Still, they managed mostly to be as happy as anyone else in the world. So what if they had to break their backs for pennies? So what if they were sometimes hungry? So what if so many Christians hated them? God willing, they believed, and with the help of such a man as Rabbi Loew, they would all live and be well.

But Rabbi Loew worried. He was only a man, and he could help the Jews only as much as one man could. Day and night he prayed for help and searched his books for an answer. Lamps burned late in his library.

"What can I do, what can I do?"

He decided to ask the mightiest power of all.

In his sleep, he directed a dream question to heaven.

The answer came in the form of several Hebrew letters that made no sense in themselves.

He awoke and immediately went back to his books. After many books and much study, he understood the message at last.

"Aha!" he exclaimed.

The letters, now words, revealed to him how to help the Jews of Prague.

Rabbi Loew would make a creature that looked like a man but was not a man. The creature would not exactly be alive like a person, but neither would he be dead. The creature would hear, but not speak. He would move, but only when commanded to. He would do just what he was told. He would be big and extremely strong.

Such a being, only partly like a human, was called a Golem. Now the rabbi knew how to make one.

The Golem would help him help the Jews of Prague.

That night, for the first time in a long, long while, Rabbi Loew fell into a deep, peaceful sleep.

CHAPTER TWO

The Golem Is Created

T he day after his dream, Rabbi Loew called his two greatest students to his house—Isaac Sampson and Jacob Sasson. First he swore them to secrecy. Then he told them of his plan to create a Golem to help and protect the Jews of Prague.

The two men agreed to do whatever the rabbi asked.

Very early one morning, long before first light, the three men quietly left their houses and met in the night-filled ghetto square. Jacob carried a bundle under his arm. The rabbi held the Torah scroll from the synagogue.

Silently, the three walked to the River Moldau. They followed the clay bank until the rabbi spoke. "Here."

It looked no different to Jacob and Isaac than any other part. But there they stopped, and set to work.

With their bare hands, they picked up clay

and pushed it together to form a shape. Gradually, as if coming from the earth itself, a figure took form. Complete with arms and legs, head and hands and feet, there lay before them a clay figure of a huge man lying on his back, his eyes closed as if in sleep.

"Isaac." The rabbi instructed him to circle the shape seven times, from right to left, and told him the formulas to whisper as he walked.

When Isaac had finished, the figure turned glowing red, as though on fire.

"Jacob." The rabbi then also instructed him to circle the shape seven times, but from left to right, and gave him the formulas he was to recite.

When Jacob was finished, the figure darkened and steam poured from the clay, as if water had been poured on flames. While the men watched, hair slowly sprouted from its head, and nails grew on its fingers and toes.

"Rabbi!" Jacob and Isaac backed away in fright.

"Shh. Don't be afraid. Wait."

The rabbi moved closer and bent over the figure. On its clay forehead he wrote the Hebrew word for Truth—EMET.

"Now," he said to the two men.

With the rabbi in the lead, holding the Torah in his two hands, the three danced slowly around the figure. Seven times they circled the formed clay lying on the earth. They then bowed

to the four corners of the world. The rabbi spoke directly to the figure:

"The Lord God formed man from the dust of the earth, and breathed the spirit of life into its nostrils, and man became a living creature."

Blood seemed to flow through the clay, which became like skin. The shape took on the look of human flesh. Suddenly, its eyes opened. They looked directly at Rabbi Loew, hard and dark. The rabbi shivered.

The Golem was alive.

"Stand up!" the rabbi commanded.

Clumsy, half falling, the Golem got to his feet. He towered over the three men. His eyes never left Rabbi Loew's face.

"Golem," Rabbi Loew said, "understand that we created you for one reason only—to help and protect the Jews. Do you understand?"

The Golem nodded.

"You can hear, but you cannot speak. It is better so. Because you look like a man and walk like a man, but you are not a man. You will remain forever not complete. Do you understand?" the rabbi repeated.

The Golem's eyes seemed to flare. He nodded again.

"You have been granted great powers," the rabbi went on, "powers that no human being can possess. But you will use them only for the sake of the Jews."

The Golem understood.

"Last, you will never forget that you are my servant," the rabbi continued. "If I tell you to go through fire, you will go and not be burned. If I ask you to enter water, you will enter and not be drowned. You will always do exactly what you are told."

The Golem had heard.

"Golem, bend to me." The creature leaned forward and the rabbi touched his forehead. "Of all the world," he said, "only we three men will see the Truth that makes you live."

The letters glowed, then turned pale as flesh.

"I name you Joseph, after a creature half human and half demon who did much to help the Jews in ancient times.

"Now," the rabbi said, "you will dress in the clothes Jacob carries in his bundle. They are shabby but clean. I will tell people that I found you wandering homeless in the streets, a mute of simple mind, and gave you a home with me as my servant."

With that morning's rising sun, four men returned to the ghetto from which three had left just hours before.

CHAPTER THREE

Too Much of a Good Thing

By the time the rabbi returned to his house, his wife was making breakfast. Her name was Pearl.

"Oy!" she shrieked at the sight of the silent Golem. "Who is that!"

"What's to be afraid?" he said, and told her his story of how he had found Joseph. "So, my Pearl," he ended, "Joseph will stay here in the kitchen with you until I need him. It will be better if only I command him. Because he is of simple mind, he will do only exactly what he is told to do."

A stool was placed in the corner of the kitchen. There Joseph sat silent and not moving, waiting to be called.

Now, Pearl had understood the rabbi very well. But one day she saw that the water kegs were empty. It was cold outside, and she did not like the thought of going to the well.

"What harm," she thought, "if I tell Joseph to fill the water kegs? After all, it's for the rabbi's meals."

So she handed Joseph two buckets and said to him: "Bring water from the well and put it into the kegs." She went off to another part of the house and left the Golem to do as he was told.

He did what he was told, all right. He went to the well, filled the two buckets with water, brought them back to the kitchen, and poured it into the kegs. Then he went back to the well, filled the two buckets with water, brought them back to the kitchen, and poured it into the kegs. After that he went back to the well, filled the two buckets with water, brought them back to the kitchen, and poured it into the kegs. Again he went back to the well . . .

By this time the kegs were full to the brim. But Joseph kept going back to the well and bringing more water. Soon the kegs spilled over onto the floor. Then the water overflowed and went out the door into the courtyard. Soon the water was ankle-deep. It rose up to the doorsills of the homes lined along the courtyard's sides. And still Joseph kept going back to the well.

People ran out of their doors. They splashed through water, slipping and falling, trying to catch objects that were beginning to float.

"What?" people cried.

"It's not raining!"

"The sun is shining!"

"What's happening?"

Joseph kept right on filling and emptying the two buckets.

"Help!" someone yelled. "Help! Get the rabbi!"

The rabbi came running.

When he saw the water pouring out of his own kitchen door, he understood what had happened. He went quickly to the well, where Joseph was filling two more buckets.

"Enough water!" the rabbi said. "Stop! The kegs are full. Go back to your seat!"

Joseph silently returned to the kitchen and sat down on his stool.

The rabbi went to his wife. "Some helper you got yourself," he said to her. "Soon we would need Noah and the Ark."

Pearl tried to explain that since the water was for the rabbi, well then she thought—

"Only me is he to obey," the rabbi said. "That's the first thing. The second thing—what a pity you didn't tell him to stop when the kegs were full. Because what did I tell you? Joseph will do exactly what he is told to do. An ocean you would have had here. Now will you remember? And not use him as your helper again?"

Pearl nodded, shamefaced, and went to mop up the kitchen floor.

CHAPTER FOUR

The Red Beards

The rabbi was in the synagogue, reading the prayers that usher in the beginning of Passover. He knew the prayers by heart, but he always read them from the page. He said that the shape of the letters each time gave the prayers new and deeper meaning.

He made a mistake.

Instead of "and He changes the seasons," out of his mouth came "and He *sours* the seasons."

He tried it again. "Sours" came out a second time.

"Ai!" he thought in fright. "This must mean something terrible is to happen."

He told the congregation to continue praying and not to leave until he gave the word. He sent the same instruction to all other synagogues in Prague.

The Golem was needed. He was at the rabbi's side in a wink.

"Go to my house and bring back two pieces of matzo—one the regular kind, and the other the special kind baked only for Passover."

The Golem vanished, then returned in two winks.

"Here," Rabbi Loew said, "taste." He broke off a piece of the regular matzo and handed it to Joseph. He chewed it up and swallowed, then nodded and rubbed his stomach.

"So. It is good. Now," said the rabbi, breaking off a piece of the special matzo, "another taste."

Joseph put the matzo in his mouth and instantly his face turned pale. His features twisted and he clutched his stomach, bent over as if in terrible pain.

The rabbi placed his hands on Joseph and the pain vanished as if by magic.

The congregation by this time was loud with fear.

"Jews!" the rabbi said. "Hear me! The matzo prepared for Passover is declared forbidden to eat. Send word to all synagogues, to all the Jews of Prague. I will find out what has happened here!"

He summoned all the people who had been involved with the baking of the Passover matzos and asked if anyone not Jewish had worked with them.

"Yes." A small Jew with a long beard

stepped forward. "On the last day, we were afraid they would not be ready in time. So we asked two Christian baker's apprentices to help us. What else could we do?"

"Quick! What are their names?"

"I—I don't know, Rabbi."

"Who knows among you?"

A woman spoke up. "Each had a red beard. So we called them the Red Beards. What else could we call them?"

"Shah—be still! Send word to all Jews that yesterday's matzos are banned, but all others are fit to eat."

They left, and the rabbi summoned the Golem.

"Joseph, go to the house of the Red Beards. Look carefully. If you find any suspicious vials of liquid or packets of powder, bring them to me. Now, go!"

The Red Beards were not at home, and Joseph had no difficulty in his search. He returned to the rabbi in a twinkling, holding a little box in his hands.

The box held a fine powder. It was half empty.

The rabbi sniffed the powder. "The smell is the same as the corrupted matzos, only stronger. Yes, yes, Joseph, this is the poison. Return it to the Red Beards' house, exactly where you found it."

It didn't take long for the Golem to do just that and once again stand at the rabbi's side.

The rabbi called his helper, Abraham Chayim, and the leaders of the community to join him. They moaned and clutched their heads in fear and worry.

"Rabbi, what's happening?"

"Who tried to kill us?"

"Is the matzo all right, Rabbi?"

"Rabbi, Rabbi, why are we being punished?"

"Ask no questions now. Come with me."

Out they went into the night. Swiftly they walked through the dark streets. The rabbi led, the Golem by his side.

They went through the gates of the ghetto and continued walking.

"Oy, Rabbi, this is not allowed. Where are we going? Where?"

"What, all of a sudden you don't trust me? To Christians also is murder a sin. All will be well. All."

Along the way they passed the two Red Beards. They looked very surprised to see a group of Jews rushing so outside the ghetto, and so much after dark. The Golem turned his head and glanced at them. They fled.

The one lighted building at that time of night was the police station. The group went straight inside. The rabbi asked for the chief of police.

He did not mention the box of powder, and he did not tell what the Golem had done. He talked only about the matzos and what he had learned.

All agreed that the finger of guilt pointed to the Red Beards.

"I will investigate," the chief said.

With a few of his men, he went off to the Red Beards' house.

As the Jews left the station, Rabbi Loew whispered to the Golem: "Go—find the Red Beards. And bring them to where the police will find them."

With that, the Jews went home to their families to celebrate the first night of Passover.

The Golem—who knows how—found the Red Beards racing out of the city as fast as they could go. He snatched them up, put one over each shoulder like a sack of potatoes, and brought them back to Prague.

He dumped them in front of their house, just as the police were coming out to look for them. For the police had found the box of powder and recognized it as poison.

Thoroughly bewildered and frightened— they thought their punishment had already begun with the Golem—they confessed their evil deed right away. They were sent to prison for many years, and no one heard of them again.

And so the Golem had helped Rabbi Loew save the Jews of Prague from a terrible misfortune during Passover, the very Festival of Deliverance.

CHAPTER FIVE

The Butcher

It was true that Rabbi Loew feared most for the Jews' safety during Passover. All too many Christians believed that Jews murdered an innocent Gentile child or a pure woman every year at this time. Such people believed the Jews drank the blood during the Seder, or else added it to the matzo dough. Since Jews are forbidden to consume blood, this was the most monstrous lie of all. It was called the Blood Libel.

Those with the deepest hatred of Jews would sometimes hide a dead child's body in the ghetto. When it was discovered, they would cry "Proof! The Jews are murderers!" If it was found in a house, the Jews living there would go to jail or even be executed. If the corpse was in a public place, then — oh, woe, woe! — gangs would raid the ghetto in a pogrom, killing Jews on sight.

In this, as in other matters, the rabbi made good use of the Golem.

As Passover approached, he called the Golem to him.

"Joseph," he said, "tonight and every night until I tell you different, you will not sleep. Go out into the streets. Watch everything around you with great care. If you see someone carrying a bundle, or a wagon carrying a load at an hour when all decent people are in their beds, investigate carefully. If you find a dead body, take the corpse and person straight to the police. Let nothing stop you. Do you understand?"

The Golem nodded. He went out into the streets of the ghetto, and this is what happened.

One of the leaders of the Jewish community—a wealthy man, may his luck stay golden—had lent a large sum of money to a Christian butcher. He did not repay one penny, and the Jew was about to take him to court.

The butcher burned with hatred for the Jew, because he knew he could not pay him back. A plan to land him in prison grew in the butcher's mind.

He went to the cemetery and found the new grave of a Gentile child who had just died. By the light of the moon, he dug up the body. With his knife, he slit its throat so the corpse would look slaughtered. Carefully he wrapped it in a tallis, the Jewish fringed prayer shawl. This bundle he placed inside the body of a dead pig he had put in his cart, and covered it with a sack.

The butcher went off to the ghetto. He planned to leave the child's poor corpse in the Jew's basement, where surely it would be found and result in the Jew's imprisonment.

The ghetto was black with night. The moon had gone in, and it was as if all the lamps in the world had gone out.

But the Golem could see what he needed to see.

Swift as light, he was beside the cart.

The butcher almost fainted with fright. "Who are you? Where did you come from?"

Joseph pointed at the bundle in the back of the cart.

"What do you want with that? That's mine. What are you doing? Stop it. Stop!"

The Golem had found the tallis-wrapped child's body.

The butcher shrank in fear. "What's that? It's not mine. I had only the pig. Someone put it there!"

Joseph made it clear the butcher was to come with him.

"I'm not going anywhere. What do you want with me? I'm just a poor man. Leave me alone!"

He punched the Golem.

The fight that followed was something to see, if anyone had been there to see it. The butcher was no weakling. But the Golem was most certainly stronger.

In moments, the butcher lay bruised and bleeding. He stopped fighting.

Joseph threw him in the back of the cart. He took wagon, butcher, pig and body on his back, straight to the steps of the police station. There he dumped the load.

This job done, he returned to the ghetto.

The butcher groaned and cried out, as much in fear as anything else. The police rushed out to see. Getting no sensible answer from the butcher, they searched the wagon and found the body. When they saw the tallis, they understood instantly that the butcher had planned a false blood accusation against the Jews.

He was immediately arrested and sent to jail for a long time.

Rabbi Loew, who knew all secrets, decreed that when the butcher came out, he would not have to pay back the loan.

"Who knows? Maybe this charitable act will help change his mind about the Jews. After all," he said smiling only a little, "anything is possible. Yes?"

CHAPTER SIX

The Ruin

An old building, a gunpowder factory years before, stood at the very edge of the ghetto. Long empty, it had fallen into decay. The ruin's vacant windows looked like blank black eyes staring inward. Nothing good lived there.

The Jews believed the structure haunted by evil spirits. Some swore they had heard the sound of military band music late at night. One man said he saw a soldier on the roof playing a trumpet. Others had seen dozens of black dogs running in a silent circle around the outside of the building.

No one willingly walked by the ruin, especially not after dark. But one night, a Jewish courier hurrying home absentmindedly passed right by the entrance.

Out of nowhere a large black dog flew at him. Barking ferociously, it ran around him in circles, then disappeared inside the building.

The courier arrived home still shaking with shock and horror. After telling his family what had happened, he went to bed hoping for a peaceful sleep.

Later that night, his family woke up to hear barking in the house. They had no dog, so what was this?

They found the man, now awake, covered with sweat and white with fear. He had had a terrible nightmare.

He dreamed that he was riding with a group of soldiers. All of them, including himself, were mounted on the backs of large black dogs. When the dogs barked, so did the soldiers. They threatened to throw the courier into the ruin unless he barked along with them. That was the sound the family had heard.

His wife comforted him—after all, it was just a dream—and told him to go back to sleep.

It was only the beginning.

Every night, the courier had the same nightmare. And every night, his own barking awoke him in terror.

He grew afraid to sleep, his bed a place of torture. But sleep he must, even if only a doze, and when he did, the dream returned.

Weeks went by. Nothing changed. Exhausted, he grew weak and sickly. Finally he was unable to work. Poverty loomed, another nightmare.

With his family, he went to see Rabbi Loew and asked for his help.

The rabbi listened with sympathy. "Let us

try to find out why you are being so tormented, for I know you are a good man."

Rabbi Loew inspected the man's tallis katan, the small fringed prayer shawl very pious men wore under their clothes at all times. Two corner fringes had been torn off.

Next he carefully examined his phylacteries, the two small leather boxes that held verses from the Bible. There too he found a blemish.

"So. Here is why. Your greatest shields against evil are damaged. These we will repair."

He told the courier to cleanse himself at the mikveh, the ritual bath. Then for seven nights he was to sleep in Joseph's bed, and Joseph would lie in his. The rabbi gave the courier a magic amulet. This he would put on after sundown and not remove until morning light.

And so it happened. The Golem went each night to the courier's house and lay in his bed dreamlessly. The courier lay in Joseph's cot, and by the sixth night, the nightmare had faded to dim lines and faint sounds. By the seventh, the dream was gone.

The Golem, having done his part, went back to his cot. The courier returned home, a rested and happy man.

More remained to be done.

Rabbi Loew called Joseph to him.

"Here are two bundles of straw and a torch. Go to the ruin and set it on fire so that its evil will not haunt or harm Jews ever again."

The Golem went away to do as he was told. Many hours went by. The Golem did not return. First curious, then wondering, then worrying, the rabbi left his study and went into the street. He could see the glow of the fire coming from the direction of the ruin.

Joseph had done his job. But where was he?

Rabbi Loew raced through the maze of darkened streets to the building.

"Oh God!"

The ruin was ablaze. Leaps of flame shot from every window and through the collapsed roof. Black smoke billowed from reddened cracks in the brick. Boards fell in showers of brilliant sparks.

And there, in the midst of the heat from hell, stood the Golem. Fire was everywhere. But he did not burn. For the space around him was bare of flame and clear of smoke.

"Joseph!" the rabbi called.

The Golem did not move.

"Joseph! Quickly! Come out!"

The front of the building crashed into the street, the flames reaching toward the rabbi.

The rabbi spoke in Hebrew. "Golem! I command thee! Come to me now. I am thy master!"

The Golem turned his head. He looked at Rabbi Loew with eyes that glowed huge with unnameable light. They seemed liquid, as though he was weeping.

The next moment he stood beside the rabbi,

unburned, untouched, his eyes no different from the obedient creature Rabbi Loew had made.

"Come, Joseph. Now we will go home. You have done what you were told."

The courier dreamed no more of barking black dogs. The Jews of the ghetto were freed from the evil of the ruin. But Rabbi Loew was left with much to think about.

CHAPTER SEVEN

The Priest

There lived in the ghetto a widower, whose daughter Dina had brought him little but heartache. Raised without a mother, at fifteen she ignored her father and did as she pleased. She seemed to loathe the well-meaning Jews who tried to give her guidance, and at times did things just out of spite. Her father finally gave up trying to control her.

Therefore he did not know that she was secretly seeing the priest Thaddeus.

The priest was a notorious anti-Semite. His hatred of the Jews knew no limits. Many believed him behind the Red Beards' attempt to poison the Passover matzos a few years before. It was said he pulled out his hair when the butcher's plot to leave a corpse in a Jewish house was foiled.

He charmed Dina. He brought her everything she asked for, from chocolates to foods she never dreamed of tasting. He told her she was beautiful, and gave her jewelry and clothes that she modeled before him while he exclaimed over her loveliness.

Small surprise, then, that Dina decided to convert to his religion.

This filled Thaddeus with joy. Not for love of Christianity, no, but because of his mad hatred of the Jews. Thaddeus had a plan to get rid of Rabbi Loew and the cursed mute who was his servant once and for all.

Some months before this, a Gentile servant woman in a Jewish home disappeared. Her employer assumed that she had returned to her home village and gave it no further thought. In truth, no one knew where she had gone. Thaddeus put her disappearance to good use.

Before Dina could be accepted as a convert, she would be questioned by the cardinal of Prague regarding her reasons. Thaddeus instructed her carefully. Now completely under the priest's control, she hated Jews and her Jewishness, and agreed gleefully to do as he said.

"Why do you wish to leave the Jewish faith?" the cardinal asked.

"Because Judaism is barbaric, and I wish to have no part of it."

"Why do you say it is barbaric?"

"Because the Jews slaughter Christians and use the blood in their religious rituals."

"How do you know this?"

"Because shortly before Passover, the mute who works for Rabbi Loew and another who could speak came to my father's house late at night and gave him two vials filled with blood."

"How do you know it was blood?"

"Because the one who could speak said to my father, 'The rabbi sends you Christian blood for Passover,' and the mute nodded."

"And then?"

"My father gave them a large contribution for the rabbi, and later told our cook to empty one vial into the dough for the matzos, and the other into the wine. It sickened me so, I decided to leave the faith forever."

The cardinal was an intelligent man and no Jew hater. He was more than suspicious and pursued his questioning. "Where," he asked, "did this blood come from?"

"I cannot be certain. But I heard the speaking one whisper to my father: 'Next year, another Christian servant will supply us with blood again.' The mute only smiled."

The cardinal did not believe one word of this tale. But since he had no proof it was not true, he was obliged to report it to the authorities. He had great respect for Rabbi Loew and sent him a secret message with Dina's story, saying that only if the missing servant woman was found alive would the tale be proven false.

Rabbi Loew read the message with horror.

He knew they would jail Abraham Chayim and also come for Joseph. It was likely he too would be put in jail sooner or later. There would be a trial. Unless some witness proved the story a lie, Jew haters would fall on the ghetto like beasts in a wild rampage of bloodshed and destruction.

But who would be a witness for the truth? The girl's father, no doubt in shame over his daughter, had left Prague for another country. That left the Gentile servant woman. She must be found.

Rabbi Loew acted quickly.

He assured the thoroughly frightened Abraham Chayim that, with God's help and a little luck, he would not be in jail for long.

He dictated a letter for the servant woman's mistress to sign and kept it with him.

He had a homeless mute brought to him from the streets, a tall, big man. The rabbi knew Dina had rarely seen Joseph and barely knew what he looked like. Most Jews had seen little of him and only briefly, since he stayed mainly in the rabbi's house. Those outside the ghetto had never knowingly clapped eyes on him. One poor mute was the same as another to all of them.

The mute who stood before him, truly simpleminded, was content to be warm and fed with a roof over his head. He agreed happily to do whatever the rabbi wanted.

The rabbi dressed him in Joseph's clothes and left him in Joseph's place.

He called the Golem to him.

"Joseph," he said, "would you recognize the Gentile servant woman?"

Joseph nodded.

"She must be found, or catastrophe will befall the Jews. Here is a letter from her former mistress, promising her easier work and more money if she will return. I have myself added money to the envelope. Give this to the woman, and she will go with you. Bring her back here. Find her, Joseph!"

The Golem left.

All then happened as the rabbi knew. Abraham Chayim was arrested, as was the mute in Joseph's place. A trial date was set. The rabbi was told to be present.

Days passed. Joseph did not return.

The Jews of the ghetto, terribly worried and frightened, prayed day and night.

Weeks went by, and Joseph did not come back.

The day of the trial neared. Rabbi Loew called for special services in all the synagogues of Prague.

No Joseph.

The morning of the trial arrived. Where was the Golem?

A mob had gathered outside the courthouse, not a Jew among them.

A carriage pulled up. When Thaddeus and the girl emerged, the crowd cheered wildly. The priest nodded to the right and to the left and entered the building smiling, the girl on his arm.

Soon another carriage appeared. When Rabbi Loew stepped out, an animal roar of rage came from the mob. Shouts filled the air.

"Filthy Jew!"

"Jew pig!"

"Jewish murderer!"

"Kill him!"

Stones began to fly. Without the police to protect him, the rabbi would not have made it to the entrance alive.

The courtroom was packed, Jews on one side, Christians on the other.

A bell announced the start of the trial. The emperor's attorney read the charges. Abraham Chayim was questioned first.

"Did you murder a Christian woman and use her blood in your religion?"

Abraham Chayim answered in a strong voice. "No, sir. I did not."

Thaddeus stood up. "Why would he not lie?"

"Sit down," said the judge.

The mute, present as Joseph, was next. The

attorney showed him two vials filled with blood-red liquid. "Do you know what this is?"

The mute smiled, licked his lips, and rubbed his stomach.

Thaddeus jumped to his feet. "There! You see? He admits his guilt!"

"Sit down," repeated the judge.

The lawyer for the defense rose. "Prove his guilt? Not at all. This simple man may think the liquid is wine and would taste good."

The Jews in the courtroom laughed. The others murmured angrily.

"Quiet!" said the judge.

"I will ask him in another way," the defense attorney went on.

He took a knife from his pocket. Tilting back his head, he held the blade to his throat while pointing first to the blood-red vials and then to Rabbi Loew. In this way he suggested murder and tried to make the other connections clear.

The mute turned white and trembled. He shook his head so hard his earlocks flew.

Thaddeus leaped up. "He thinks you ask if the rabbi should be killed! He is afraid of the rabbi's power. Surely you see his fear!"

An uproar in the courtroom followed. Thaddeus and the lawyer shouted at each other, the audience yelled their comments and opinions, and the judge tried to create order.

Rabbi Loew stood up, and the Jews quieted. The others soon calmed down as well.

Dina, the chief witness, was called to give her testimony. Her voice edged with triumph, she repeated the same unspeakable story she had told the cardinal.

The attorney asked, "Do you see the rabbi's servants here in the courtroom?"

She laughed out loud and pointed at Abraham Chayim and the mute. "I would know them in the dark!"

A tense silence filled the courtroom.

Suddenly there was a commotion from outside.

"Find out what that is," ordered the judge.

A wagon raced wildly through the crowd. The driver lashed out left and right with his whip to get screaming people out of the way.

It was Joseph. Beside him sat the servant woman.

He rushed with her immediately into the courtroom and went straight to Rabbi Loew. He bowed his head. All had happened as the rabbi said. The Golem had finally found the woman in a hamlet long miles from Prague, and she agreed to go with him as soon as she read the letter.

"What," the judge asked in some exasperation, "is happening here?"

Rabbi Loew rose from his seat and explained what he had done.

"So," he said, "the truth is now revealed."

And so it was. All charges against the Jews were dropped. The girl was sentenced to six years for giving false testimony. No one noticed Thaddeus sneak out in silence.

A good home was found for the mute. The servant woman was content in her work. Rabbi Loew sang prayers of thanksgiving. The Jews of Prague were at peace. And the Golem returned to his place in the rabbi's kitchen.

CHAPTER EIGHT

Fish and Apples

Rosh Hashanah, the New Year, was the occasion for a great feast at the rabbi's house. Pearl, his wife, was running around like a nervous chicken to get everything done in time. Suddenly she realized that she had neglected to get the fish for the meal.

"Woe is me!"

Then she remembered that she hadn't gotten the apples yet either.

"*Gevalt!*"

She could spare none of her helpers, or else other things would not be ready. She went to the rabbi and asked him to tell Joseph to go to the fishmonger and the fruit vendor.

"After all, husband, it is for a worthy reason," she said, "for what is Rosh Hashanah without fish and fruit?"

Rabbi Loew agreed. He gave the Golem instructions, handed him notes for the sellers, and told him to make haste.

Off the Golem went to the market.

First, the fish.

The fishmonger selected a large carp — it must have weighed at least twenty pounds, and still alive — and wanted to put it in a sack. But the Golem had been told to hurry. So he snatched the fish from the seller and went off.

The fish was very busy moving and was slippery besides. Joseph had trouble holding it in his bare hands. He slipped it into his shirt and tightened the belt.

The fish's head was down, his tail up next to Joseph's face. And that tail moved back and forth, back and forth.

The fish gave Joseph such a hard slap in his face with its tail that it knocked him to the ground.

The Golem could not forgive the fish that slap.

He went, full speed, to the river and threw the fish into the water with such tremendous force that it sank to the bottom and disappeared.

So. No fish.

Next, the apples.

The fruit vendor weighed out the correct amount. It was a large order. She too wanted to put the fruit in a sack.

Shaking his head, the Golem pulled on the

woman's arm and pointed at the pile of apples.
He wanted to carry them in his arms and be off
right away.

"What, suddenly you're a juggler?" She
laughed at him. "Look at this one," she called
out. "He thinks he can juggle apples faster than
the eye can see." The sellers in the nearby stands
saw the mound of apples, and they too were
laughing at Joseph.

The Golem flew into a rage.

Quick as a flash, he picked up the woman,
together with her stand and all the baskets of
fruit. He placed the lot on his shoulders and carried it all swiftly through the streets. The woman
screamed the whole while, but not one of the
amazed witnesses of the sight could stop him.

He arrived at the rabbi's courtyard. There
he set down the stand and vendor. Then he went
inside the rabbi's kitchen and sat in his usual
place.

"You're here?" said Pearl. She looked
around. "And the fish? The apples? They're
where?"

Joseph gestured toward the courtyard.

Pearl went to see. Her eyes fell on an unbe-
lievable sight.

A crowd had followed the Golem and his
unusual load. They came streaming into the
courtyard, which was by now packed with people.

The fruit vendor, deciding the adventure shouldn't be a total loss, was back in business. She was selling her fruit right and left. Right there in the rabbi's courtyard.

The rabbi came home, a little out of breath. He had heard what had happened with the fish. He soon saw what had happened with the apples.

He laughed. "Well, so she'll start the New Year a little richer than in the old."

When the baskets were empty, he told Joseph, he was to return the stand to its proper place. He was not, added the rabbi, not to carry the vendor. She would walk with him to the market.

The New Year feast that night was merrier than usual. True, they had no fish to eat. But of apples they had plenty!

CHAPTER NINE

A Bad Exchange

In Prague at the time there were two good friends named Berel. One had red hair, the other black, so they were called Red Berel and Black Berel. They grew up together, married at about the same time, and became successful business partners. Their wives also became the best of friends. In time, the two families had many children between them.

And that's where the one big difference between them came to be.

Red Berel's wife had several handsome sons and beautiful daughters, all born healthy and strong. But Black Berel—ah, his sons and daughters were born pale and sickly. The Angel of Death visited that house all too often, leaving only one small daughter alive.

Now, both women had been helped to give birth by the same midwife. Her name was Esther. Being a midwife, she heard many secrets. And the grief and heartbreak of Black Berel's wife were well known to her. She felt deep pity and wanted greatly to help her somehow. Soon enough, her opportunity came.

It happened that each of the wives became pregnant at the same time. Almost as though by plan, both delivered the same day.

Black Berel's wife gave birth to a boy, sickly and silent. Red Berel's wife also gave birth to a boy, but healthy and howling.

Esther switched the babies, right after they were born.

"Congratulations," she said to Red Berel. "You have a son."

"Congratulations," she said to Black Berel. "You have a son—and this time, you are blessed with a healthy one."

Esther told not a living soul what she had done. And no one was the wiser.

The boys grew up, each with the wrong mother and father. With luck and much care, both became healthy, handsome, and brilliant.

Some years passed. Esther died suddenly, taking her secret to the grave. When Black Berel's only son was the right age, it was decided that he would marry Red Berel's daughter. A large wedding with a huge feast was planned. Rabbi Loew agreed to perform the ceremony, which was held in the courtyard of the synagogue.

The courtyard was absolutely stuffed with

Jews, for the Berels were important people in the ghetto. The crowd watched in quiet joy as Rabbi Loew stood under the bridal canopy and raised the goblet of wine. He began the blessing.

"Blessed art Thou—"

The goblet fell from his hand and the wine spilled onto the ground. The crowd groaned.

The goblet was refilled, the rabbi raised it, and began a second time to recite the blessing.

"Blessed art Thou—"

Again the goblet dropped from his hand and the wine spilled.

The rabbi froze. The crowd fell stone silent. This had never happened before. Never.

Rabbi Loew wanted to try a third time, but the flask was empty. The Golem was sent to the rabbi's house, across the street from the synagogue, to replenish the wine. At the entrance, he stopped. His head cocked, he seemed to be listening to someone. He went into the rabbi's study instead of to the wine cellar, where he was seen through the window to write something down.

The crowd in the courtyard moved aside and watched, whispering with curiosity, as he walked to the bridal canopy and handed Rabbi Loew the piece of paper.

Rabbi Loew read: "The bride and groom are brother and sister."

The paper almost flew from his hands. "Joseph!" he cried. "Who told you this?"

Joseph pointed to the topmost synagogue window, as though something behind it had spoken to him.

The crowd looked, and most saw nothing, although later some said they had seen the window glow. The rabbi looked, and nodded as though all his questions had been answered. He turned to the crowd and said, "The wedding must be postponed until this matter is looked into with great care. Give the food for the wedding feast to the poor."

The next morning, Rabbi Loew told all who came to the synagogue to stay after their prayers as witnesses to what would follow. He ordered a table set up beside the *bimah,* the platform in the center of the synagogue from which the Torah was read. He brought two rabbinical judges to sit beside him. All three were wrapped in their prayer shawls and wore phylacteries. At his instruction a screen was set up in a corner to his left. He then sent for Red and Black Berel and their wives, along with — may all be spared such a match — the bride and groom.

"We three," he explained, "will judge this matter carefully. Now, parents, tell us of your lives."

The two Berels and their wives spoke a long time, telling all they could remember of their lives.

"There is no blame here," Rabbi Loew said

after they had spoken. He called the Golem to him.

"Joseph," he said, "go to the graveyard and bring the spirit of the dead midwife Esther here to the synagogue." Joseph left, swift as wind.

The people cried out in terror. "Don't be afraid," the rabbi said calmly. "Nothing here will hurt you. It is only the truth we seek."

Joseph reappeared. He pointed to the screen. Behind it was a light that moved restlessly up and down, back and forth. The sound of a woman weeping carried into the room.

"Who are you?" asked the rabbi.

"I am the spirit of Esther the midwife," a distant voice behind the screen answered.

"Why are you here?"

"In the twelve years since I died, I have been allowed no peace because of what I have done. I would be sent to suffer in the farthest edges of Gehenna if this marriage had been performed. Because of your great virtue, Rabbi— may your name be blessed—your servant was permitted to summon me here from the dead to prevent the great sin from happening. The bride and groom are brother and sister. It is all my doing."

"Explain," ordered Rabbi Loew.

The three rabbis and the two families heard the explanation. All others heard only a soft whispering sound from behind the screen.

The families moaned and wept as the midwife's spirit told her tale.

"That is what I have done," the spirit ended. "Believe me, I only meant well. Who could not weep at Black Berel's tragedies? Only a heart of stone. Aiee! Now I will never rest."

"The Master of the World does not lack compassion. Suffering spirit, what is needed to bring you rest?"

"Forgiveness. From those I have wronged. Only forgiveness."

"Brother and sister, who have been saved from grave sin," Rabbi Loew said, "do you forgive Esther the midwife for her grievous mistake?"

They spoke as one voice. "We forgive you, Esther the midwife."

The three rabbis said together, "Spirit, go in peace and rest in peace until all is peace."

The light behind the screen vanished on a sigh.

The rabbi called for the community book of records and briefly wrote the full story, which was then signed by all present. It is believed to this day that the document waits only to be found.

So it ended. But not yet. For then it happened that the son who had returned to his father married the daughter of the other Berel, who had grown up with him. And this wedding was a ceremony of exceptional joy.

"Without the Golem," Rabbi Loew said to himself, "who knows what would have taken place here? I did well to have created him, did I not?"

CHAPTER TEN

The Attack

Some years before the Golem came to be, a Jewish family named Nadler traveled to Prague from Spain. Their ancestors, along with many others, had become Christians to save themselves from being burned at the stake—for where in that terrible time was any Jew safe? Now in the company of those who shared the ancient faith, they returned to Judaism with joy. They lived pious lives of charity and virtue.

The ghetto did not accept them easily. They looked a little different from those around them. Also, they wore different clothes, ate somewhat different food, followed slightly different daily and religious customs, and prayed in a different-sounding Hebrew from the Prague Jews. Because those with their name had once been forced to become Christians, gossipers said behind their hands that Jewish blood did not flow pure in their veins.

Eventually the family moved on—perhaps

to Russia, although some swore Germany—but
the evil idea remained and grew. Whenever a
Jew of Prague wanted to insult anyone, he called
him "nadler," meaning his Jewish blood was im-
pure. The insult was a terrible one. Moreover, it
was unjust, since the namesake family was blame-
less.

Rabbi Loew spoke out against the habit. A
virtuous history was being defamed, a worth-
while name corrupted, and an innocent family
mocked. But the custom grew, until even little
children taunted playmates with cries of "Nadler,
nadler!"

He called together a rabbinical council and,
with the burning of two black candles and at the
blast of the shofar, the hollow horn of a ram, the
use of the insult was banned.

The word was rarely heard thereafter. But
three low-minded bullies continued to use "nadler" to anger people and to start fights.

The rabbi found out about this, of course,
and asked to see their leader. This man, a porter
by trade, laughed and said he would come as
soon as he felt like it.

The Golem was sent to bring him. He tossed
the porter over his shoulder and carried him like
a bleating lamb through the streets to the rabbi's
court. There he was forced to listen to long lec-
tures on disobedience without moving even a

hair, and made to go barefoot to Rabbi Loew and ask his forgiveness.

The three bullies never used the word again. But the porter burned with rage, especially at the Golem. He determined to pay Joseph back for the humiliating ride through the ghetto over his shoulder. With his two friends, the porter devised a plan.

After every Sabbath, the Golem refilled the rabbi's water pitcher at a particular deep well. The three hid until he arrived. When Joseph leaned over to raise the water bucket, they grabbed his legs and tipped him into the well.

Joseph went in with a great splash. The three looked down and laughed at what they saw.

Joseph flailed wildly about on the water's surface. He grabbed at the sides of the well, but the slippery stones threw him back into the water each time.

"Look—a fish!" one cried.

"No—a duck! A stupid duck!"

"Ha—a boat. A sinking boat! It goes straight to the bottom. Watch!"

With that, the three threw heavy rocks down onto Joseph's head. When he ducked beneath the surface, they thought him drowning and left him there. Bruises and bloody gashes he surely had, but the Golem did not sink.

Night fell, and when Joseph did not return,

the rabbi sent men to look for him. Joseph heard them from inside the well, and began to splash and clap his hands together to make the only sounds he could.

They clutched each other in fear.

"What's that, what's that?"

"A demon!"

"Save us!"

Joseph splashed louder and clapped harder.

They finally had the wit to lower a lantern into the well, where they saw Joseph's wet and bleeding face. With the aid of his great strength and all their efforts, they managed to pull the Golem up out of the well with the bucket and rope. They brought him to the rabbi.

He blanched at the sight. "Investigation later. First, dry clothes and warmth." That accomplished, he touched the Golem's wounds with his hands and they healed.

"Now, Joseph, tell me—who did this to you?"

With gestures and motions, Joseph made himself understood.

"Ah," said the rabbi. "This cannot be allowed. Joseph, you stay here. The villain who did this to you will have a surprise."

The next day the rabbi sent two men to visit the porter. However they did it, it was done, and he arrived at the rabbi's unsuspecting.

At the sight of the Golem, he shook. "But he drowned!"

"Thus do you reveal your guilt," said the rabbi. "Joseph, we will leave you with him. Do only what is just."

The Golem fell to with a vengeance.

He punched, he kicked, he pounded, he picked him up and threw him against the wall. In short, he went after the porter like a slaughterer to a bull.

Studying in the next room, the rabbi shook his head at the bangings and thumpings. He gripped the arms of his chair at the howls of pain. He stood up when the howls turned to screams for mercy. When the screams turned to sobbing, he rushed into the room.

"Enough! Stop!"

The Golem dropped the porter like a sack and stood silent.

"Take him home," the rabbi instructed the men who had brought him. "Let him be nursed back to health. The needed lesson he has learned too well." The porter was wrapped in blankets and carried away.

"Joseph," the rabbi said, "this was a man, not an animal. Even animals are not to be tortured. What have you done?"

Joseph did not move.

"Golem, hear me. True justice permits mercy. And revenge is forever forbidden."

But of justice the Golem understood nothing. No more did he know of mercy, nor of revenge.

The Golem did not move.

"Ai, Joseph. You have strength and power. It is what I asked of you. No more than these could I expect." The rabbi sighed deeply. "Go now to your place."

The Golem left the room.

"I have done this," Rabbi Loew whispered. "What, indeed, have I done?"

CHAPTER ELEVEN

The Five-Sided Palace

The story here is one of blood and murder. Hatred is its root. In hatred there is evil, and in evil there is madness. That is the lesson, if there is one. And that is why the story will be told.

To begin, then.

Right across the street from the synagogue there stood a strange building. It was called the Five-Sided Palace. Such a name does not come from nowhere, and this building deserved what it came to be called. For one, it stood where five streets met. For another, there were of course five sides to the building. Yet more, each of the sides contained five pillars, and between each pillar there were five windows.

The building was ancient, so old that the worn carvings along its sides were thought to be from the days when people worshiped the sun. Some early Christian kings of old Prague had lived there at one time too.

No one owned the building anymore, not the government and absolutely not the Jews. It was crumbling, falling into ruin.

In rooms that had not yet collapsed, homeless beggars lived as best they could. Even the lowliest among them would not descend into the cellar, because they swore demons lurked there. If by accident they gave the smallest look at the black hole that led downward into its depths, they shuddered and quickly spat three times to ward off its evil.

Passover of this fateful year began no differently from any other. Every last crumb of leavened bread had been sought out and removed from even the poorest Jewish homes. The special matzo was prepared. Jews everywhere readied themselves for the Festival of Deliverance, the Festival of Freedom that marked the Ancient Israelites' escape from the Pharaoh, may his name be blotted out.

Rabbi Loew was in the synagogue about to read the prayer affirming the removal of the leaven. He read by the light of a candle.

Suddenly the candle went out.

Abraham Chayim relit the candle, and the rabbi began over.

Again it went out.

It was lit three times, four, and always as if from an unnoticed breath, the flame died.

The rabbi paled, and the people in the synagogue murmured in alarm.

The rabbi instructed Abraham Chayim to read the prayer out loud by the light of the wall sconce, and the rabbi would repeat it after him.

Prayer book in his hands, Abraham Chayim began: "All the leaven I have . . ." But instead of "have," out came the word *"five."*

He almost dropped the prayer book.

"Again. Begin," said Rabbi Loew.

In a voice shaking with fear, nonetheless the word from his mouth was *"five."*

"Ah. Now I understand," said the rabbi. "Terrible misfortune threatens us. They wish to extinguish our light, the light of the Jews, for they wish to extinguish us. But first—" He took the book from Abraham Chayim's trembling hands, and, standing close to the wall sconce, he read the prayer without mistake to the end.

By this time the women were weeping and the men moaning in distress.

"Jews!" Rabbi Loew said. "Do not be frightened. Tell everyone who hears of this that I will investigate and all will be made clear. For have I ever failed you? Go now to your homes. Passover is a time of rejoicing, not sorrow, and so it must be."

He asked Abraham Chayim to remain and called the Golem to him.

"The other night," the rabbi said, "a terrible dream came to me. The Five-Sided Palace was on fire. It burned with such fierceness that its flames reached out to burn the synagogue, which was packed with Jews. A horror, a horror." He shook his head.

"Then I did not comprehend the dream's meaning. Now I do. Something there in the Five-Sided Palace threatens our very light, our very lives. Abraham Chayim, what do you know of the men who live there?"

"Rabbi, not all are good men nor are all honest. They are Jews, if not exactly good Jews. But none are evil. Our peril does not lie with them."

"It is as I thought. Joseph," he said to the Golem, "you have eyes where most men cannot see. Take us to the foul root of our danger. We must destroy it before it can destroy us."

Enveloped in the silent darkness of midnight, they left the synagogue for the Five-Sided Palace. Rainy damp air blew in their faces as they approached its entrance. Once within, their only light came from the three braided candles they took with them from the synagogue.

Joseph brought them to the black hole that led to the cellar. Wooden steps, half rotted and broken with decay, led downward into unknown space. Joseph pointed exactly there, and Rabbi Loew peered within.

The smell of the tomb rose to meet him. As he straightened in disgust, all three heard the sound of whining. At first it was like the whimper of a child, then rose to the sound of barking dogs, finally to a sound like the unceasing roar of some beast unknown to normal light and life.

"Rabbi, it is true—it is the Other Side! We dare not go there, we dare not!" Terror spoke from Abraham Chayim's mouth.

"Sh!" replied the rabbi. "We must try. The lives of Jews—perhaps the light of Torah itself, erase the thought!—depend on us this night. Come. We will see what there is to see."

The three began to descend. The steps seemed to break away from their feet, while the odor of the grave and the whining and roaring grew and swirled around them.

Finally they stood at the bottom. "Joseph," Rabbi Loew said, his own voice—may it be admitted?—shaking perhaps a little from fright, "Joseph, go forward. We will follow."

As Joseph moved into the darkness, stones began to fall from the ceiling onto the rabbi and Abraham Chayim. For their lives' sakes they stood still.

"Joseph," Rabbi Loew called again, "you have the strength and courage of ten. Go where we cannot go without dire harm. If anything lies there that would bring affliction to the Jews, bring it here to me."

The Golem vanished into the darkness, and in moments he returned.

He carried a basket in one hand and a small bundle in the other.

The basket held several vials filled with thick red liquid. Each vial was labeled in Hebrew with the name of a leading Jew in the ghetto, including Rabbi Loew. The bundle, opened, revealed the corpse of a little girl, her throat slit and all blood drained from her body.

Rabbi Loew saw and cried out in anguish. "How could this be? Who could have done this? How could this hideous wickedness be brought here unseen, unnoticed, unfound?" He wept.

"Ai, Rabbi, I'm such a fool!" said Abraham Chayim suddenly, striking his forehead.

"You say this now?"

"Rabbi, when I was a child we were told that once a king lived in this palace. He wanted no one to see him—who knows why? So he had a hidden tunnel dug here—right here in this cellar—so he could visit his priest without being seen. Rabbi, my own mother—may peace be upon her—told me the tunnel leads directly to the church."

"Thaddeus's church." Rabbi Loew wept no more.

"Yes, Rabbi. The priest."

"At last he is mad. Joseph," he directed, "dig a deep hole, place the vials there, and smash them all. Bury them so that they may never be found. You understand?"

The Golem nodded.

"Then, Joseph, find the tunnel. Take this slaughtered little one and there, in the cellar of the church, hide her body. Only, be sure to hide it so that someone can find it. But not right away. Not today, not tomorrow, but in three or four days' time, someone should be able to discover the body. Do you understand this, Joseph?"

The Golem understood, and did what was asked of him.

When he returned, the three left that place of horrors. Safe in their homes, they awaited the turn of events.

Early the next morning, great numbers of policemen entered the ghetto. At their head was the chief of police. Beside him, almost hugging his side, was the priest Thaddeus.

The house of every Jew whose name had been on a vial of blood was entered and searched thoroughly, especially the rabbi's house. Of course nothing was found, and those watching noticed that the priest's face turned a little redder each time the police emerged empty-handed.

When they passed the Five-Sided Palace, Thaddeus grabbed the police chief's arm and whispered in his ear while gesturing toward the structure.

The police went into the building, threw out

the bewildered beggars, and inspected the place
from top to bottom. Even the cellar, which they
treated like any other, was gone over inch by
inch. Not so much as a suspicious shadow did
they find.

The chief of police wore an angry look, and
Thaddeus, now pale, was seen to bow in apology.

Jews flooded Rabbi Loew with worried
questions. He calmed them all, saying: "Jews, be
comforted. God's help will protect you." For he
knew, this knower of secrets, what was to come
and what had happened to bring it about.

The period of Passover for the Jews brought
Easter for the Christians. The priest Thaddeus
ordered his servant to see if more wine was
needed. The servant went down into the deepest
church cellar where the wine was stored. There
in the torch-lit gloom, he noticed a half-hidden
bundle. He unwrapped it.

It was the butchered body of his own child.

A scream tore from his lungs.

There are no words, and will be none here,
to tell of his agony.

The police were soon informed of everything
that had occurred.

A few weeks earlier, the servant and his wife
had been working in Thaddeus's walled garden.
Their children played nearby. The youngest
child, a girl, wandered a little way off. There
Thaddeus found her, and there grew the first foul

seed of his plot against the Jews. For the child had no reason to suspect the priest, who was no stranger to her, and went with him gladly.

Thaddeus murdered her and filled the marked vials with her blood. He was by then so maddened with glee at what he had planned, and so filled with hidden horror at what he had done, that he forgot—actually forgot—to place the vials in the Jews' homes. Yet in his madness, he believed he had done so. Thus had the Golem found body and blood together.

Thaddeus told the worried parents that their child must have wandered away, which was true enough, and no doubt would wander back sooner or later.

"But on second thought," said Thaddeus, and then went on to say that perhaps there was some reason to worry. Passover was coming and Jews—well, the Jews were known to take an innocent Christian's life and use his or her blood in their rituals. It was a fact, the priest told them, that Rabbi Loew and other Jewish leaders took the most for themselves.

If the child did not return in another day, the priest advised them, the parents should report her missing. In order to spare them further suffering, he, Thaddeus, would go with them and aid the police in their investigation.

All then happened as has been told.

Thaddeus was arrested. In wild rage at being discovered, he not only confessed to the murder, he also gave details of what he had planned against the Jews. Thaddeus was put on trial, found guilty, and sentenced to a lifetime's imprisonment. He was defrocked, forbidden as unworthy to carry out his priestly duties.

Thaddeus's actions, his trial and conviction were the talk of Prague, Jews and Christians alike. The emperor himself was kept informed. The priest's trial proved once and for all that the Blood Libel was wretched slander from start to finish, and always had been. Because of this, the emperor decreed that the charge could never again be made and, further, that anyone caught spreading the lie would be imprisoned.

There was much cheering and celebration among the Jews of Prague. Prayers of thanksgiving rose from all the synagogues.

"All of this joy," thought Rabbi Loew, "became possible because of the Golem. Without him, who knows? I am content with what I have done here."

But this story does not yet end, not quite. More of importance took place.

As Thaddeus was being taken away in shackles, he tore loose from the men holding him and made a speech that the watching Jews told to their children, and their children's children heard of it, and down through the years until no one believed it anymore except as a tale to frighten those who misbehaved or refused to study.

"Jews!" said Thaddeus. "Jews, you hear me now. You are rid of me. I am gone from your lives. But that is for now, and for now only.

"For I will return. Believe me, I will return and you will not recognize me. I will tell the same stories, I will tell the same lies. Those who listen will hear them as the truth. Lies become truth when they are believed, Jews, and you will not have known pain until those days come.

"The murders will be of you, do you hear me? All of you! You will suffer, be tortured, you will die. You will burn, burn as if in the ovens of hell. You will matter less than ashes, no more than smoke.

"Your God is no army, your faith is no shield. For I will return in uncounted numbers to destroy you. That is my promise!

"Jews! Do not forget!"

He was dragged away.

When told of this, Rabbi Loew said, "He is mad, and despite what he has done deserves our pity. But there have been people like Thaddeus before, and there will be many others like him again. Why should our future be so different from our past?"

He sighed deeply. "We can only pray that the worst of his curses do not come to pass. Is a world without Jews possible, God forbid?"

Out of nowhere, appearing like a message, he saw in his mind the Golem standing unburned in the flaming ruin, protected in the midst of fire.

He smiled.

"Ach. A way will be found, always. We have endured this long, have we not? And so we shall continue.

"Yes. God willing, the Jews will survive."

CHAPTER TWELVE

The Golem Runs Amok

The Jews of the ghetto did not have to worry about the Blood Libel anymore. A few fools thrown in jail brought that story to an end. At least, in Prague. For the time being.

Other than that — not a small thing! — ghetto life went on much the same as before.

The Jews who were poor did not get any richer. Could they make gold from straw?

Hungry Jews did not suddenly get fat. Does bread come from a stone?

Christians did not out of nowhere greet them with open loving arms. What, the Jews should drop dead from shock?

In other words, the emperor was no Joshua, Prague was no Jericho, and the ghetto walls did not come tumbling down.

Even so, they managed mostly to be as happy as anyone else in the world. With God's help, they believed, and with the wisdom of such a man as Rabbi Loew, they would all live and be well. Had the rabbi himself not proved it ten times over?

The rabbi went about the daily business of being who he was. He inspired students with his learning and understanding. With the mind of a Solomon, he helped solve the problems that were brought to him from people near and far. He presided at joy-filled weddings and brought solace at many deaths. Festivals were happier than ever. His piety increased, if such a thing was possible, and his praying sang to the heavens.

And the Golem? What of him?

Now that the worst threats were past, there was of course less for him to do. No longer did he have to roam the nighttime streets to seek out evildoers and Jew haters. His special powers were put to use when needed, but this took place less often than in earlier years. It was Joseph who knocked on the shutters of Jewish homes to remind the faithful that it was time to pray. He chopped wood for the stoves, brought water from the wells—just enough, not too much. When he was not seated on his stool in the kitchen, he helped in many small matters of a rabbi's daily life. Between him and Abraham Chayim, the synagogue was never so clean nor so well prepared for all services and prayers.

Now, Joseph was a Jewish golem—what else would he be? But because he was not completely human, there were many religious laws he did not have to observe. So it was with the Sabbath.

For religious Jews, the Sabbath is the holiest day of all the days. It is when the Creator rested, and Jews too must rest. Further, it is a foretaste of the World to Come. No work is permitted. Only prayer, love, peace, and tranquillity are to be their lot during that brief span.

Every week, therefore, just before the start of the Sabbath at Friday sundown, Rabbi Loew told Joseph what he was to do until the end of the Sabbath at sundown Saturday. This was done, because to tell the Golem on the Sabbath day what work to do was itself work, and this was prohibited.

The rabbi, however, was only human. So on one Friday—it had to happen sooner or later—he simply forgot to tell the Golem how to keep himself busy. He did not even remember to tell Joseph to remain on his stool. A terrible mistake.

The synagogues of the ghetto were full. In almost every house, candles lit especially for the time shone warmly. Glowing white tablecloths awaited the Sabbath meal that would be eaten with gladness and thanks.

Rabbi Loew, like the others, was praying in his synagogue. The Sabbath had already been ushered in with the psalm sung for the occasion.

There was a commotion at the entrance. Cries of surprise and distress arose from those assembled. Through the crowd stumbled a man, his clothes torn and blood running down his face. He came directly to the rabbi.

"What has happened to you?" Rabbi Loew exclaimed.

"Rabbi, Joseph has run amok!"

"What? Explain!"

"He was in the streets. Others tell me he walked with no purpose, like a child on an empty afternoon."

"Yes? Yes? And then?"

"Rabbi, he has gone mad! He picked up carts and threw them. He tore down doors and signs. He smashed wagons to splinters. May my eyes never see it, I heard he pulled apart a horse limb from limb. All who tried to stop him were kicked away. Some were thrown like blocks of wood against walls. He grasped a cripple by his beard and hurled him down stone steps."

"Rabbi, save us!"

Rabbi Loew took a step toward the door and then stopped as if frozen.

"But I can do nothing," he lamented. "The Sabbath has begun. To control Joseph profanes the day. What can I do, what can I do?"

He rocked with dismay, and then looked at the bleeding bearer of the message.

"No. I am wrong. The Law commands that human life is holier even than the Sabbath."

He rushed through the crowd to the steps of

the synagogue. There he spoke in a voice like a lion's roar:

"Joseph! Stop where you are!"

Then he spoke again. "Joseph! Come to me now!"

In moments the Golem stood before him.

The rabbi said gently, "Go to your usual place. I will call for you when you are needed."

As though nothing had happened, the Golem turned and walked away to the rabbi's kitchen.

Rabbi Loew went back inside the synagogue. "Come," he said to all those present, "let us repeat the Sabbath psalm and begin the holiest and most peaceful of days."

Much later that night, after the Sabbath meal had been eaten and the songs sung, Rabbi Loew arose sleepless from his bed and went to his study. He knew he should not think of troubling things on the Sabbath, but his worry kept him in his chair.

There in the darkness he sat and thought long and longer about what had happened and about this creature he had made.

"He is obedient like a machine, but he is no machine. He seems like a man, but he is not a man.

"He does not know justice, or mercy. He cannot know love, or feel it. Charity he cannot perform. Human beings were given these virtues, so that they could choose not to behave like beasts.

"But what does the Golem know? Does he know his own power? His strength?

"No. He cannot know anything he is not told. Except, his strength and power can lead him to violence, to savagery.

"Therefore he must always be controlled, or else he goes out of control.

"Who must control him? I must control him.

"Will I live forever? No, I will not."

He struck his breast. "I have created a life, thinking to be like God. But human is all that I am, so the creation is flawed. Being mortal, I have failed as fail I must.

"I believed it was needed for my people's sake. But I was blind to the needs of my own pride.

"I can only pray to be forgiven."

By the time first light appeared over the crowded rooftops of the ghetto, Rabbi Loew had made a decision.

CHAPTER THIRTEEN

The Death of the Golem

Soon after the Sabbath ended, Rabbi Loew asked Isaac Sampson and Jacob Sasson to his house. These were the two who had helped him create the Golem. As before, first he swore them to secrecy. Then he began to explain why he had called them.

"The Golem has done his work," he said. "The Jews of Prague are safe—well, safer than before, yes? So, then, it is time."

"Time, Rabbi?" asked Isaac Sampson.

"I am no longer young," the rabbi continued. "Who will take care of him? Who will command him? Who will control him after I am gone?"

"Rabbi! May you live to be a hundred and twenty," said Jacob Sasson.

"Yes, yes. To you the same. But the great dangers that brought forth the need for the Golem are past—"

"From your mouth to God's ears, Rabbi!"
Isaac Sampson spoke.

"Yes." The rabbi sighed. "So. The priest
Thaddeus is in prison. A royal decree protects us
from the Blood Libel. The Christians who hate us
will not so quickly defame us now. Do you begin
to see?"

The two men saw.

"Good. Listen closely to my words." He told
them what he had planned.

Jacob and Isaac agreed to do whatever the
rabbi asked.

When darkness fell, Rabbi Loew called the
Golem to him. "Joseph," he said, "tonight you
will not sleep in your usual place. Go to the synagogue, and there in the attic make your bed."

As always, he did as he was told.

Long after the ghetto slept, the three men
met. With them was old Abraham Chayim, who
knew more than he ever said, which was known
by Rabbi Loew. Abraham Chayim held two candles, the group's light as they climbed the stairs
to the attic of the synagogue.

There lay the huge figure of the Golem, his
eyes closed as if in slumber.

"Golem, you will not awaken," said Rabbi
Loew softly. "Jacob. Do what you know to do."

Jacob circled the Golem seven times, from
right to left, and whispered again the formulas
learned years before — this time, backwards.

"Isaac," said the rabbi.

He too circled the Golem seven times, from left to right, and recited the old formulas, also backwards.

Joseph's body now lay stiff, as if breath no longer moved in his chest. On his forehead, the EMET that gave him life paled.

"Now it is time," said Rabbi Loew. He bent over the body and, with gentle touch, erased the first letter.

EMET, which is Truth, became MET, which is Death.

The Golem was dead.

Silently, Abraham Chayim undressed the clay figure, leaving on only his shirt.

The shape was then covered with worn tallises and yellowed pages from old prayer books, stored as was the Jewish custom there in the synagogue attic.

The men descended without a word and went to their homes.

In the morning, the story was spread that Joseph had run off during the night and was nowhere to be found.

Secretly, Abraham Chayim burned his clothes to ashes.

Rabbi Loew announced that the use of the attic for discarded holy objects was discontinued, and that all were forbidden to go there for fear a kindled light might start a fire.

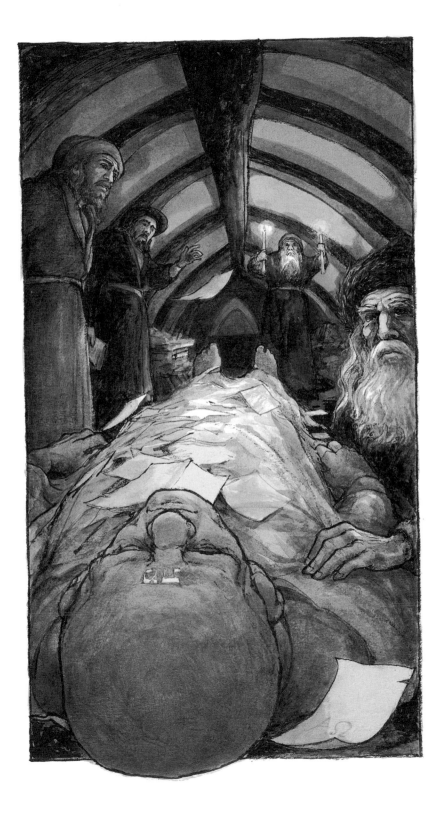

Some said the rabbi suddenly grew old. Some even said he mourned. But that could not be, for the Golem was not a human soul. It was true that the lamps again burned late in his library, where more than ever before he studied and spent long hours in prayer.

No one was ever to know that the figure of the Golem lay hidden in the attic of the synagogue.

It is said that the Golem lies there to this day.

Well, and does he?

Who knows what the truth is?

Who knows?

Author's Note

Rabbi Judah Loew was a real person. He lived from about 1512 until 1609. He was extremely pious, a learned scholar of Judaism, and a great mathematician. He became chief rabbi of Prague and established a school there, where his vast knowledge earned him many disciples. His several religious works are studied by Jews to this day. A statue of him, wearing his usual large cloak, tall hat, and long beard, presently stands before the Prague town hall.

His synagogue was called the Altneushul. One of the oldest in Europe, it remains in use in modern-day Prague.

Rabbi Loew's wife actually was named Pearl, as she is in the story. One of the men with the rabbi at the creation and death of this story's Golem has the real name of Loew's son-in-law, Isaac Sampson.

The use of the Blood Libel against the Jews is one of the terrible facts of history. It is, and has

always been, a lie. Jews are forbidden to consume blood in any form. Here, from Leviticus in
the Bible, are God's instructions: "No soul of you
shall eat blood, neither shall any stranger that
visits among you that hunts and catches any beast
or fowl that may be eaten; he shall even pour out
the creature's blood, and cover it with dust." Religious Jews have followed this to the very letter
through all the centuries since.

But the lie would not die. Some scholars
think that even the Ancient Romans believed it.
Through the ages, there have been priests, Jewish converts to Christianity who came to hate
Judaism, many among the common people, even
kings who have believed that Jews killed children or pure women in order to use their blood in
the matzo or even to drink it in their wine.

The Nazis of Germany used the lie to help in
their murder of 6 million of Europe's Jews during the Holocaust of 1933–45.

The lie lives still. In Syria, a book called *The
Matzo of Zion* warns children to be careful because a passing Jew "may take your blood to
make [Jewish] bread." In the early 1990s, a peas-
ant in Poland was asked if he believed the story.
He said, "They say now it's not true, but we have
heard stories . . ."

Emperors, popes, enlightened priests, edu-
cators—at one time or another, all have said the

belief is false. But still it lives. Only the truth can kill it. The truth, told again and again.

Did the actual Rabbi Judah Loew create a golem? No, he did not. Scholars talk a lot about why the story attached itself to him, but the most they can come up with are two theories. The story takes place during a period when Blood Libel stories had become fairly common, and many Jews were killed or jailed because of it. The two most famous versions of the legend, Yudl Rosenberg's and Chayim Bloch's, appeared in the early twentieth century, when once again Blood Libel stories were resulting in murderous pogroms. The story of the golem was thus created to give Jews hope of a protector, especially to help defend them against the terrible consequences of the ghastly lie.

But these are only theories. No one knows why Rabbi Judah Loew and the Golem have been joined in the tale.

Has there ever been a golem? The idea is certainly a very old one. Adam in the Bible is called *golem* until God breathed a soul into him that gave him the power of speech, which made him fully human. Through the centuries, stories of such a creation appear again and again. Learned rabbis were even said to have created a calf, which they then ate; another rabbi was believed to have made a golem to use as a housekeeper; others made golems that became so powerful they destroyed their maker. There have been plays about golems, movies, an opera, even a comic book. The Frankenstein monster was a kind of golem. It's possible that the golem of today is being created by humanity's growing dependence on the computer, that machine without a mind of its own—or perhaps in scientists' desire to create new forms of life in test tubes.

Thaddeus, the evil priest, appears in many versions of the legend. But he is not based on any one person. He is a combination of several, for all too often priests spoke out against Jews, calling them killers of Christ and accusing them of evil and murderous deeds. The lies told about Jews regularly resulted in pogroms, sometimes led by the priests themselves. Often Jews were forced to leave their own country. This happened in England, France, Spain, Italy, and elsewhere throughout Europe.

One other important fact: Hebrew was the religious language of the Jews. It was considered almost holy, since it was used only in prayer and in the synagogues. That's why in chapter 6, the rabbi addresses the Golem in Hebrew when all else fails. Not until Israel was founded in 1948 did Hebrew officially become an everyday language of the people.

BR

Illustrator's Note

At the time this story took place, all European Jews were required to wear the yellow circle that you see on the left shoulder or sleeve of many of the characters in this book. The yellow circle set them apart from the rest of the world. Some of the men in the pictures are still wearing the yellow-pointed hats that were another "lawful" sign of Jewishness requred in the previous century.

It's interesting to realize that the yellow Star of David or triangle that Jews were forced to wear during World War II was not an idea invented by the Nazis. This kind of "branding" had been going on for many centuries. Fashions in clothing change slowly, but human ignorance and prejudice haven't changed a bit throughout history

Based on my research, I believe the costumes and the general feeling of the Jewish community of Prague in the sixteenth century are more or less correct. But because I have never visited Prague, the landscape of the ghetto is purely from my imagination.

The Hebrew letters that appear in the small illustrations are in most cases based on the letters that the Rabbi Loew wrote on the Golem's forehead to bring him to life — emet, which spells "truth." When the first letter is erased, the remaining letters — met — spell "death." All the other letters I got from the Haggadah, which is the story of Passover used at the seder.

I don't know Hebrew, and I am in no way a scholar, so I apologize for any inaccuracies in the Hebrew letters I have drawn. However, I do know a good story when I see one, and I have tried with my pictures to give this story the touch of truth that will help the Golem live again.

TSH

Definitions

Most Jewish or religious words are defined as they are used in the story. But definitions of a few of the more difficult terms are given here.

Gehenna: The Jewish hell.

Gevalt: A Yiddish word used to express surprise, shock, pain, and deep disappointment. There is no exact definition in English.

Mikveh: A large community bath used by religious Jews for special cleansing purposes. Women use it before marriage and at certain other times, and men whenever a special cleanliness is called for. Some use the mikveh before the Sabbath, for example.

Passover: The eight-day holiday that marks Moses' deliverance of the Jews from slavery in Ancient Egypt over three thousand years ago. When the Egyptians' firstborn children were slain by God, the Israelites' homes were "passed over" and spared. Passover is also called the Festival of Deliverance or the Festival of Freedom. During the first two nights a special meal is eaten—the seder—during which the story of the escape is told and special types of food are served. The most well-known is matzo, a flat bread made only of flour and water. It stands for the speed of the Jews' escape, which was too fast to allow time for their bread to rise. During the eight days, this unleavened bread is the only kind that may be eaten.

Phylacteries: Two small square leather boxes containing biblical passages, worn on the left arm and forehead during morning weekday prayers. Called *tefillen* in Hebrew.

Shofar: A hollow ram's horn blown in the synagogue only on the highest of holidays, and to make only the most important of religious announcements.

Tallis: A prayer shawl, fringed at the bottom, worn by men and some women at prayer at religious services. The tallis katan is a smaller version, worn under the clothes at all times.

Torah: The first five books of the Bible: Genesis, Exodus, Leviticus, Numbers, Deuteronomy. They are the central sacred scriptures of Judaism.